"KAIN-NA AVA!"

Maria Avila-Gonzales

Kindle Direct Publishing

To our little beanie bear.

May you continue to explore the world with
your contagious smile, your beautiful heart, and
your unconditional love...
while enjoying good food along the way.

Ava can eat pancit every single day.

Ang sarap naman!

Lumpia is so tasty...

Maraming ang laman.

Kare-kare is a favorite...
the flavors are so robust.

Lechon kawali is so crispy...
Dinner at Lolo and Lola's is a must!

Longanisa, sinangag,
tocino, dinuguan and puto,

suka with sili, bagoong, and patis,

sinigang, adobo, sisig, and crispy pata,

whatever we're having, she can't resist ...
especially food that is matamis!

Glossary:

Adobo (sounds like: ah-doh-boh) - Filipino dish that contains pork or chicken marinated in vinegar, soy sauce, garlic, bay leaves, and black peppercorn

Ang sarap naman (sounds like: ah-ng sa-rah-p nah-mahn) - It's so delicious

Bagoong (sounds like: bah-go-oh-ng) - Sauteed shrimp paste; used as a condiment for several dishes

Crispy pata (sounds like: pah-tah) - Deep fried pork leg

Dinuguan (sounds like: din-ooo-goo-ahn) - savory stew with pork and meat simmered in a rich dark gravy of pig's blood

Kain-na (sounds like: kah-in nah) - let's eat

Kare kare (sounds like: kah-reh kah-reh) - Stew that features a thick savory peanut sauce with stewed oxtail, beef tripe and vegetables

Lechon kawali (sounds like: leh-ch-own kah-wal-ee) - Cubed, deep fried pork belly

Lola (sounds like: low-lah) - grandma

Lolo (sounds like: low-low) - grandpa

Longanisa (sounds like: long-gah-knee-sah) - filipino sausage

Lumpia (sounds like: loom-pea-ah) - filipino spring rolls with meat and/or vegetables; can be served fried or fresh

Maraming ang laman (sounds like: mah-rah-ming ah-ng lah-mahn) - Lots of filling

Matamis (sounds like: mah-ta-miss) - sweet

Pancit (sounds like: pahn-sit) - noodles; many different variations and filling

Patis (sounds like: pah-tiss) - fish sauce

Sigig (sounds like: see-sig) - chopped up pork or fish seasoned with lime or calamansi juice, onions, and chili peppers

Sili (sounds like: see-leh) - chili peppers

Sinangag (sounds like: sin-ahn-gah-g) - Filipino garlic fried rice

Sinigang (sounds like: sin-ee-gah-ng) - a sour and savory filipino soup that contains meat or fish and vegetables

Suka (sounds like: sue-ka) - vinegar

Tocino (sounds like: tow-see-no) - Filipino-style sweetened and grilled cured pork Ipsum

Made in the USA
Coppell, TX
26 June 2025

51193445R00017